Big Truck Day

Words by **Rosanne Parry**

Pictures by **Niki Stage**

Greenwillow Books, *An Imprint of* HarperCollins*Publishers*

For all of my nephews, with my loudest love:
Joe, Bob, Jonathan, Christopher, John, Nate, Noah, Daniel, Joseph, Tom, Andrew,
A.J., Alex, Henry, Vince, Tony, Nick, Zach, Eddie, George, Will, Ryan, Declan,
Fitzwilliam, Cormac, Quaid, Pierson, Lincoln, Matt, Jacob, and Owen—R. P.

To my three . . . J, A, & E—N. S.

Big Truck Day
Text copyright © 2022 by Rosanne Parry
Illustrations copyright © 2022 by Niki Stage
All rights reserved. Manufactured in Italy. For information address
HarperCollins Children's Books, a division of HarperCollins Publishers,
195 Broadway, New York, NY 10007.
www.harpercollinschildrens.com

The full-color art was created digitally using Procreate® for iPad.
The text type is Archer Medium.

Library of Congress Cataloging-in-Publication Data is available.

ISBN 978-0-06-321886-4 (hardcover)

22 23 24 25 26 RTLO 10 9 8 7 6 5 4 3 2 1
First Edition

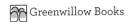 Greenwillow Books

Thanks to the following for photographs on p. 32 (left column, top to bottom): Courtesy Washington
County Free Library, Hagerstown, Maryland; National Archives, photo no. 26-G-3422; Hawai'i State
Archives, General Photographic Collection, AUTOMOBILES, PP-3-3-029; Acción Visual/Diana Arias,
CC BY-SA 3.0, via Wikimedia Commons; and (right column, top to bottom): Courtesy Bennington College
Library; Anne Arundel County Public Library, Maryland (two photographs)

Up with the sun. No time to play.

Let's all get ready for Big Truck Day.

Start at the station and fill up the tank.

Truckers have plenty of people to thank.

Suds up the scrubbers and get that rig clean.
Drivers take pride in a polished machine.

HoNK

Whoosh

Ah-oo-gah

VROOM

Uphill slow.
Downhill fast.

Turn left at the corner.

Books are for all kids,
no matter how tall.

Three cheers for the book truck!
The best truck of all.

The book wagon. Washington County, Maryland (1905-1910).

WPA pack horse librarians. Knott County, Kentucky (1938).

A bookmobile in the territory of Hawai'i (circa 1955).

Biblioburro, a traveling library in Colombia, South America (2006).

The story behind the bookmobile

Bookmobiles bring books to readers who don't live near a library. They are found around the world. In Norway, books come by boat. In Colombia, they travel by Biblioburro. Camels bring books to children in Kenya, and Laos has an elephant library.

In 1839 in the United States, Harper & Brothers created the first mobile library, a collection of books in wooden trunks designed to travel by stagecoach to far-flung schools in the West.

In the early 1900s, librarians in Maryland and South Carolina built mule-drawn wagons to bring books to families who lived far from the library.

Horses were the key ingredient in the Pack Horse Libraries, which operated through the Great Depression.

As more rural communities got roads, mobile libraries moved into converted trucks and buses. The newest, greenest innovation in mobile libraries is the book bicycle!

Watch for the bookmobile where you live. Or help create a new one!

I am grateful for the libraries and bookstores in my community. I believe all families need access to books, no matter where they live.
—Rosanne Parry

A bookmobile in Greensboro, North Carolina (circa 1936).

A very fine bookmobile owned by the New Ca. County Free Library, Delaware (undated).

Patrons visit the Anne Arundel County librar bookmobile in Maryland (undated).

A book bicycle in Westport, Connecticut (202